Grover's Own
ALPHABET

Letters by Sal Mu...

> Hello, everybodee! It is I, lovable, furry old Grover, here to make an entire alphabet for you to look at whenever you want! READY?

D1413900

A Sesame Street/Golden Press Book

Published by Western Publishing Company, Inc. in cooperation with Children's Television Workshop. © 1978 Children's Television Workshop. Grover © 1978 Muppets, Inc. All rights reserved. Printed in the U.S.A. No part of this book may be reproduced or copied in any form without written permission from the publisher. Grover is a trademark of Muppets, Inc. Sesame Street® and the Sesame Street sign are trademarks and service marks of Children's Television Workshop. GOLDEN®, GOLDEN® & DESIGN, A LITTLE GOLDEN BOOK®, and A GOLDEN BOOK® are registered trademarks of Western Publishing Company, Inc. Library of Congress Catalog Card Number: 81-84276 ISBN 0-307-01086-4/ ISBN 0-307-60190-0 (lib. bdg.)
G H I J

A

This is a little awkward, but is it not an absolutely adorable A?

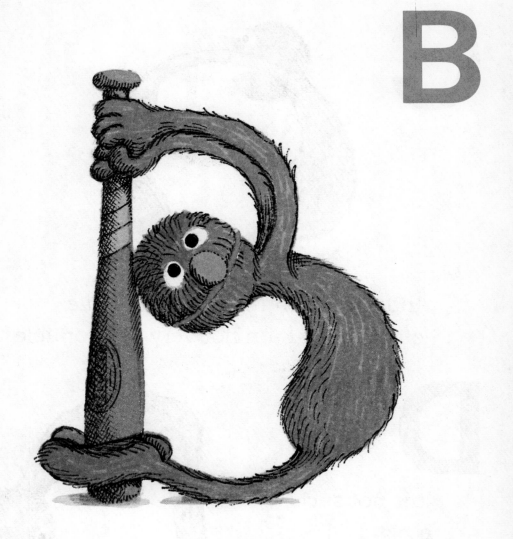

B

I bet you think making this big
beautiful B with my furry little
body is easy. Well, it is not!

C

And now I am making you a *cute*
letter C! But I am not very comfortable.

D

It is not such
a big deal
to do a D!
It is delightful!

E

I have to bend my elbow
exactly right, but how is this
for an elegant E? EEEK!

F

Here is a funny, furry F for you!

G

G is for GROVER! Watch while I,
Grover, form the great letter G!
Am I not graceful?

H

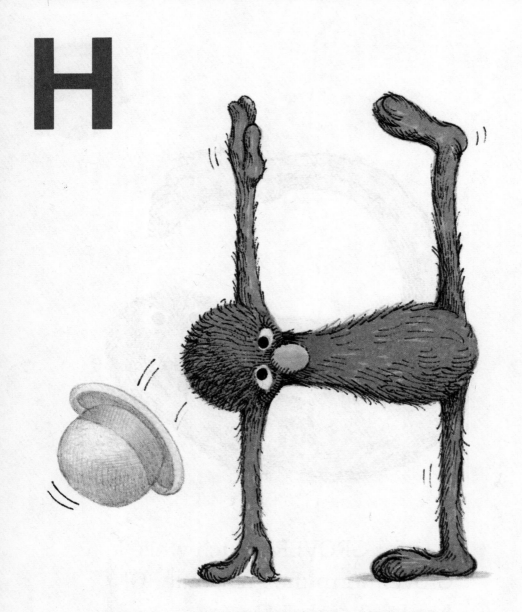

I hope this H makes you happy.
It is hard to do (pant, pant)! Help!

I

It is I, Grover, making
the important letter I.

J

Now (puff, puff!) I am juggling
just to show you a J. I could get
in a jam this way.

K

This is the letter K.
I am not kidding.

L

I do not like to be lazy about
this, but the lovely letter L
takes very little work.

M

Isn't this a magnificent M?
It is made by ME!

N

I thought we would *never* get
to the nifty letter N!

Oh, my goodness (glub, glub)! I am
not the only one in this ocean.

P

What is the point of my standing like this? I am pretending to be the letter P.

Quick! Answer this question!
What letter am I now? Q? Oh,
thank goodness you guessed it.

R

You want an R? All *right!!*
Here you are (pant, pant)!
This is getting ridiculous!

S

So sorry. I couldn't find a single thing to assist me with this S. I simply had to use my *self.*

T

I have tried to make a *terrific* T for you! But, oh, I am so tired. TA-DA!

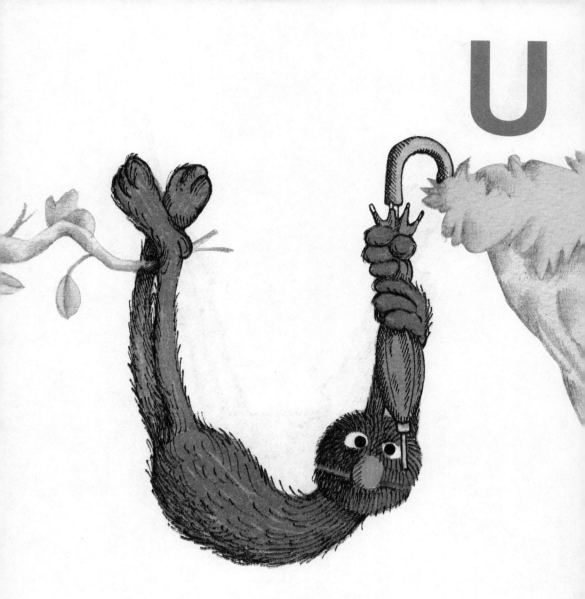

I would undergo anything
to show you the letter U.

V

You are invited to view my
very valuable letter V.

I wish you would watch
my wonderful diving W!

X

And how about this extraordinary
X? Oh, I am so excited!

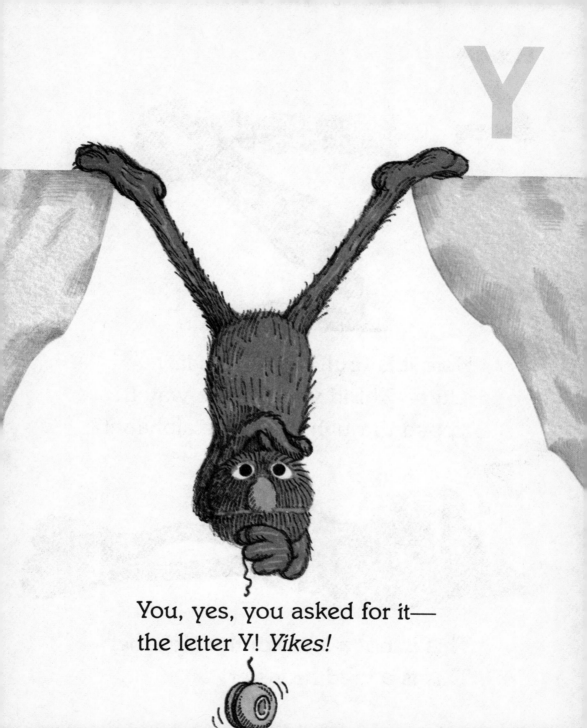

You, yes, you asked for it—
the letter Y! *Yikes!*

Z

Here it is (puff, puff!), the last letter—Z! Did you like the way I zipped through the entire alphabet?

This is not a letter of the alphabet. This is a tired monster!